# Contents

SO-BYX-652

# About the Author

A strange world of fantasy is found in the poems and stories of Edgar Allan Poe. This eerie, imaginary world was a necessary escape for Poe, for his real life was truly a miserable one.

He was born to poor parents in 1809, in Boston, Massachusetts, and was an orphan before he was three. He was taken in by his godfather, John Allan, a wealthy Virginian, who gave Poe a fine education in England and America. Then a serious quarrel with his foster father estranged him from this family while still in his teens. From then on, poverty and illness marked Poe's short life.

By the age of twenty-one, he had published three books of poems, and in 1833 a short story won $50 in a newspaper contest. His reputation grew, but his writing earned little money. He lived at that time with his aunt, Maria Clemm, a poor widow, and in 1835 he married her thirteen-year-old daughter, Virginia.

He and Virginia were often ill. His misfortunes preyed upon him, and he drank heavily. Still his years were busy, not only as a writer, but as an editor and critic as well. His ingenuous poems and intriguing short stories make him an unforgettable figure in American literature.

His poem, "The Raven," was on the lips of the entire nation after it appeared in early 1845. His horror stories still send a tingle through a reader's body today, and his detective stories set a pattern which many other writers would follow.

After Poe's wife died in 1847, Poe had what we would now call a nervous breakdown. He died in Baltimore, Maryland, in October, 1849, just forty years old.

# The Tell-Tale Heart

They Call Me Mad!

# The Tell-Tale Heart

Mad! Mad—that's what they call me.

It's true I am nervous. Very dreadfully nervous. But why do they say I am mad?

That fever I had last year—it just *sharpened* my senses—not destroyed them. Above all, my sense of hearing became the sharpest of all my senses. I heard things in Heaven and on Earth. I even heard many things in Hell. How, then, am I mad?

Listen! You will see how calmly I can tell you the whole story.

It is impossible to say how the idea first came to me, but once it entered my brain, it haunted me day and night. There was, really, no reason for the deed I had in mind—a *murder*! I loved the old man. I rented lodgings in his home. He had never wronged me. He had never insulted me. Yes, he had gold, but I had no desire for it.

I think it was his eye! Yes, it was his eye that disturbed me. You see, one of his eyes was normal, but the other resembled the eye of a vulture! It was a pale blue, with a film over it. Whenever this eye looked at me, it made my blood run cold. And so, very gradually, after much thought, I made up my mind—I would kill the old man, and then I would be rid of the eye forever.

You *do* think I am mad! But madmen are disorganized. They cannot plan anything. But you should have seen *me*! You should have seen how wisely and carefully I plotted and planned every step! And you should have seen how cunningly I went to work!

Never was I kinder to the old man than

The Vulture Eye!

during the whole week before I killed him. Every night about midnight, I turned the latch of his door and opened it—oh, so gently! And then, when it was open just wide enough for my head to fit in, I reached a dark lantern into the room. The lantern was all closed—closed so that no light shone out. Then I thrust in my head.

I moved slowly—very, very slowly, so that I would not disturb the old man's sleep. It took me an hour to place my whole head far enough inside the doorway to see him as he lay upon his bed. Ha! Would a madman have been so careful?

Then, when my head was well into the room, I opened the lantern cautiously. I opened it so cautiously that only a single thin ray of light fell upon the vulture eye. Just a single ray.

And this I did for seven long nights—every night just at midnight. But every night, I found the eye closed. So it was impossible to do my work. For, you see, it was not the old

I Open the Lantern Cautiously.

man who angered me, but his Evil Eye.

And every morning for seven mornings, when the day broke, I went boldly into the room and spoke to him. I called him by name in a hearty voice and asked how he had spent the night. So you see, he would have been a very suspicious old man, indeed, if he had imagined that every night, just at twelve, I had looked in upon him while he slept.

On the eighth night, I was even more cautious than usual in opening the door. The minute hand of a watch moves more quickly than my hand did. Not until that night did I feel the extent of my own power! To think that there I was, opening the door, little by little, and he did not even dream of my secret deeds or thoughts! I could scarcely contain my feeling of triumph. I laughed to myself at the idea . . . . Perhaps he heard me, for he moved on the bed suddenly, as if something startled him.

Now you may think that I drew back—but

A Hearty Good Morning

no! His room was completely black, in total darkness, for he always kept the shutters closed, out of fear of robbers. I knew that he could not see the opening of the door, so I kept pushing it slowly, steadily inward.

Finally I had my head in. I was just about to open the lantern when my thumb slipped upon the tin fastening. The old man sprang up in the bed.

"Who's there?" he cried out.

I kept quite still and said nothing.

For a whole hour I did not move a muscle. Yet in all that time I did not hear him lie down. He was still sitting up in bed listening—just as I had been doing, night after night, listening to the deathwatches in the wall—those tiny beetles who beat their heads against the woodwork and make ticking noises. These ticking noises are said to predict death. How right those predictions would be this time!

Soon I heard a slight groan. I could tell it was not a groan of pain or grief. Oh no! I knew

My Thumb Slips on the Lantern.

it was the groan of mortal terror. It was the low muffled sound that comes from the very bottom of a man's soul.

I knew the sound well. Many a night, just at midnight, when all the world slept, that very same groan has come up from within my own soul, deepening the terrors that I felt.

I say I knew that sound well. I knew what the old man was feeling and I pitied him, although I laughed again to myself. I knew that he had been sitting there awake ever since the first slight noise, when he had sat up in the bed. His fears had been growing upon him ever since. He must have been trying to imagine them away, but he could not. He must have been saying to himself, "It is nothing but the wind in the chimney," or "It is only a mouse crossing the floor," or "It is merely a cricket which has made a single chirp."

Yes, he was trying to reassure himself with these comforting ideas, but they were all in vain. *All in vain*. Because Death, with his

Mortal Terror!

black shadow before him, was approaching. And it was that shadow of Death that caused the old man to *feel*—although he neither saw nor heard—to *feel* the presence of my head within his room.

I waited a long time, very patiently, without hearing him lie down. So I decided to open one of the slits on the lantern just a little. You cannot imagine how silently, how stealthily I opened it until a single dim ray of light came out of the opening and fell upon his eye—his vulture eye.

The eye was open. Wide, wide open. I grew furious as I gazed upon it. I saw it distinctly—all a dull blue, with a hideous veil over it. It chilled the very marrow in my bones. I could see nothing else of the old man's face or body, because I had directed the lantern's ray precisely upon the vulture eye.

I have said before that what people mistake for madness is really the exceptional sharpness of my senses. And now my sense of

The Vulture Eye Is Wide Open.

hearing was at its sharpest. There came to my ears a low, dull, quick sound—a sound that might come from a watch that is wrapped in cotton. I knew *that* sound well too. It was the beating of the old man's heart. That beating increased my fury, just as the beating of a drum increases the courage of a soldier.

But still I remained motionless, scarcely breathing. I held the lantern without moving. I tried to see how steadily I could keep the ray shining upon the vulture eye.

Meanwhile, the hellish beating of the old man's heart increased. Every instant it grew quicker and quicker, louder and louder. The old man's terror must have been extreme!

The beating grew louder, I say, louder at every moment! And now, at the dead hour of the night, amid the dreadful silence of that old house, this strange noise excited me to uncontrollable terror.

I have said before that I am nervous; so I am. Yet for some minutes longer I stood quite

The Ray Shines upon the Vulture Eye.

still. But the beating grew louder, louder! I thought the old man's heart would surely burst. And now a new terror siezed me—would the sound grow so loud to be heard by a neighbor? Without delaying another moment I made the decision—the old man's hour had come!

With a loud yell, I threw open all the slits of the lantern and leaped into the room.

He shrieked once, only once. In an instant I pulled him to the floor and dragged the heavy mattress over him. I then smiled joyously, for the deed was done.

But for many minutes, the heart beat on with a muffled sound. This, however, did not bother me. I knew it would not be heard through the wall. Finally the beating stopped. The old man was dead.

I moved the mattress away and examined the corpse. Yes, he was stone, stone dead. I placed my hand upon the heart and held it there for many minutes. There was no beat. He

The Deed Is Done.

was certainly stone dead. His eye would trouble me no more.

If you are still thinking that I am mad, you will not think so any more—not when I describe the wise precautions I took to conceal the body.

I pried up three planks from the floor of the room and placed the corpse under the boards, in the space between the floor and the lower story of the house. Then I replaced the floor planks carefully, so that no human eye—not even *his*—could have detected anything wrong. I put the mattress back on the bed and made up the bed to appear as if no one had slept in it.

The night was nearly over, and I worked hastily, but in silence. By the time I was done, it was four o'clock, but still dark as midnight.

As the church bell sounded the hour, there came a knocking at the street door. With a light heart, I went down to open it, for what had I now to fear?

Replacing the Floor Planks Carefully

Three men stood there. They introduced themselves with great politeness as police officers.

"A shriek was heard by a neighbor during the night," one of them explained. "This neighbor suspected foul play and had come to the police office. We were sent to search the building."

I smiled at them, for what had I to fear?

"Come in, come in," I welcomed the officers. "The shriek? Oh dear—I'm sorry anyone was disturbed. That was—myself. A dream, you know. Nightmare. All right now."

Thus talking, I led my visitors through the house.

"The old man—away, you know. Gone to rest in the country for a few days. But come and see for yourselves."

I took my visitors all over the house. I told them to search—search *well*.

Finally I led them to *his* room. I showed them his treasures, secure and undisturbed.

Police Officers at the Door

Full of confidence, I brought chairs into this room and told the officers to rest *here* after their labor. I, myself, was feeling so bold because of my perfect triumph that I placed my own seat upon the spot—the very spot on the floor under which rested the old man's corpse.

I was amazingly at ease. The officers were satisfied. My *manner* had so convinced them of my story that they sat and chatted of familiar things, and I answered cheerily.

But after a while, I began to wish they would go. My head ached, and I thought I heard a ringing noise in my ears.

Still they sat and chatted. The ringing in my ears continued and became more distinct. To get rid of the ringing I talked more freely. But the ringing continued and got louder and louder, until at last I realized that the noise was *not* in my ears. What could I do?

I grew very pale, but I talked even more freely, and in a louder voice. Yet the sound

Chatting of Familiar Things

increased. It was *a low, dull, quick sound—a sound that might come from a watch that is wrapped in cotton.*

I gasped for breath—and yet it seemed the officers heard nothing. I talked more quickly, more loudly. But the noise increased steadily. I stood up and argued about an unimportant matter, argued in a high-pitched voice and with violent gestures. But the noise steadily increased. Why *wouldn't* those officers leave?

I paced the floor to and fro with heavy strides, pretending to be excited to a fury by the unimportant matter we had been discussing. But the noise steadily increased. Oh God! What *could* I do?

I foamed—I raved—I swore. I picked up the chair upon which I had been sitting and swung it about so that it grated upon the floor boards. But the noise of the chair grating upon the floor boards was drowned out by the *other* noise as it continually increased. It grew louder—louder—LOUDER!

Arguing About an Unimportant Matter

And still the men chatted pleasantly. And still the men smiled. Was it possible they heard nothing? Almighty God! No, no! They heard! They suspected! They *knew*! They were making a mockery of my horror!

That is what I thought at the time, and that is what I still think today. But oh, my agony! Anything would be better than this agony! Anything would be easier to bear than their mockery! I couldn't stand their mocking smiles any longer! I felt that I had to scream or die!

And now the noise came again! Listen— Louder! Louder! LOUDER!

"Villains!" I shrieked at the police officers. "Do not pretend to me any longer! Do not mock me any more! I admit everything! Tear up the planks—here, *here*! It is the beating of his hideous heart!"

"I Admit Everything!"

# The Cask of Amontillado

The Descendant of a Noble Family

# The Cask of Amontillado

Like my friend Fortunato, I, Montresor, was Italian and the descendant of a noble family. Did I say Fortunato was my friend? No, he was more of a rival—insulting, haughty, and always trying to show his superiority.

The thousand injuries done to me by Fortunato I bore as I best could. But when he insulted me, I swore I would get *revenge*.

Do not imagine, however, that I said a single threatening word to him. No, I kept my plan to myself. I would choose a time when I could get back at him without taking any risk. For I felt

39

THE CASK OF AMONTILLADO

I could not really be avenged if I had to suffer in some way at the same time. And Fortunato would have to know that I was repaying him for his insult. Otherwise, he would not know that this was my way of getting revenge.

In the meantime, neither my words nor my actions would show Fortunato my intentions. I continued in my usual way, smiling in his face, and he never guessed that my smile now was at the thought of how I would take my revenge on him.

Fortunato was a man to be respected, and even feared, but he had one weak point. He took unusual pride in his knowledge and appreciation of fine wine.

I was very like him in this way. I knew the wines of my country very well and, like him, I bought the best whenever I could. Because I came from a wealthy family, I was well able to afford this luxury. My treasures, in their bottles and barrels, were kept secluded in a vault in the cellar of my spacious home.

Montresor's Wine Cellar

# THE CASK OF AMONTILLADO

One evening at dusk, I came upon my friend. It was Carnival season, when everyone was feasting and drinking in a final celebration before the six-week fast that would end at Easter. In our city, everyone went quite mad during Carnival, forgetting their cares and even their dignity. Like many others, Fortunato was in costume, but I recognized him anyway. He wore a jester's outfit of multi-colored stripes, and on his head was a double-pointed hat with bells.

He greeted me with great warmth, for he had been drinking much. I was so pleased to see him that I grasped his hand and kept shaking it.

I said to him, "My dear Fortunato! How well you look! But I have exciting news. I have just bought a great cask of wine, an enormous barrel. The dealer assured me it was Amontillado, but now I have my doubts."

Of course, we both knew that Amontillado was a sherry, a particularly fine wine, made

Meeting Fortunato During Carnival

near the town of Montilla in the South of
Spain.

"Impossible!" he said. "Amontillado? At
Carnival time?"

"I have my doubts," I replied. "And I was
silly enough to pay the full Amontillado price
without consulting you in the matter, even
though I know you are the expert at such
things. But you were not to be found, and I
was fearful of losing a bargain."

"Amontillado!" he repeated.

"I have my doubts," I said, knowing I was
baiting him into my trap. "But I must be sure,
and since you are busy, I am going to Luchesi.
If anyone is a judge of wines, it is he. He will
tell me . . . ."

"Luchesi cannot tell Amontillado from
ordinary sherry," Fortunato shouted angrily.
He was rising to my bait.

"Yet there are some who say that his taste is
a match for your own," I continued.

"Come, let us go," said Fortunato.

I Bait Fortunato.

I had him now. "Where?" I asked.

"To your vaults."

"No, my friend, no. I will not impose upon your good nature. You are at Carnival. You are busy. Luchesi . . . ."

"I am not that busy. Come."

"My friend, no. The vaults are terribly damp, and I see you have a bad cold."

"Let us go, nevertheless. My cold doesn't matter. Amontillado! Surely you have been fooled. And as for Luchesi, he cannot tell ordinary sherry from Amontillado."

Still talking, Fortunato took hold of my arm. I let him hurry me along.

We reached my home, but the servants were not there. They had gone off to make merry in honor of Carnival. When I left, I had told them that I would not be back until the next morning, but I had given them strict orders not to leave the house. I knew very well that as soon as my back was turned, they would disappear immediately to go to Carnival.

"Let Us Go."

Taking two torches, I gave one to Fortunato
and led him through several connecting rooms
until we came to the archway at the entrance
to the wine vaults. As we went down a long,
winding staircase, I cautioned him to watch
his footing as he followed me.

He walked unsteadily, and the bells on his
cap jingled with each step.

After we had walked in silence through a
long, dark passageway, he asked, "The
Amontillado?"

"It is farther on," I said.

Finally, we reached the end of the
passageway and stood together on the damp
ground of the cellar—the ground that covered
the tombs of my ancestors, the Montresors.

"See how damp these walls are," I
remarked.

"Ugh! Ugh! Ugh!" coughed my poor friend,
his eyes watering from too much wine.

"How long have you had that cough?" I
asked.

Torches to Light the Way

Still coughing, he found it impossible to reply for several minutes.

"It is nothing," he said at last.

"Come," I said firmly. "We will go back. Your health is precious. You are rich, respected, admired, and beloved. You are a man who would be missed if something happened to you. It is too damp here. We will go back. You will be ill, and I cannot be responsible. Besides, there is Luchesi . . . ."

"Enough!" he said. "The cough is a mere nothing. It will not kill me. I shall not die of a cough."

"True, true," I agreed. "And indeed, I did not intend to alarm you unnecessarily. But you should be careful. Here! A few sips of this will protect us from the dampness."

As I said this, I took a bottle from a long row of similar bottles.

"Drink," I said, presenting him with the wine.

He raised it to his lips with an evil look.

"Drink."

Then he paused and nodded to me familiarly, while his bells jingled.

"I drink," he said, "to your buried ancestors who rest here around us."

"And I drink to your long life," I added.

He took my arm, and we continued.

"These vaults," he said, "are very extensive."

"The Montresors," I replied, "were a great and numerous family."

"What is your coat of arms?"

"A huge human foot, golden, against a blue background. The foot is crushing a serpent whose fangs are imbedded in the heel."

"And what is the motto on your family's coat of arms?"

"*Nemo me impune lacessit!*—let him who would offend me beware!"

The wine sparkled in his eyes, and his bells jingled as he walked. We passed into the innermost recesses of the vaults—the catacombs where human bones were piled high against

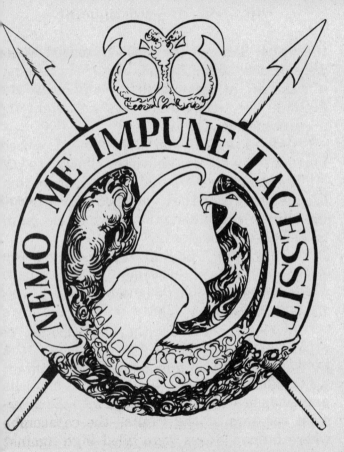

"Let Him Who Would Offend Me Beware!"

the walls. Some of my most treasured wines were next to them. I kept them there because it was cool in these vaults so far below the ground. The temperature was just right for preserving fine wines.

I paused again, and this time I seized Fortunato by his arm above the elbow.

"The dampness!" I said. "See, it increases. We are lower than the river's bed. The drops of moisture trickle among the bones. Come, let us go back. Your cough . . . ."

"It is nothing," he said. "Let us go on. But first, another sip of this wine."

He emptied the bottle in one gulp. His eyes flashed with a fierce light.

"Now let us proceed to the Amontillado," he cried.

"So be it," I said and again offered him my arm. He leaned upon it heavily.

We passed through a range of low arches and, descending again, we arrived at a deep crypt or burial room. Here, the air was so foul

Cool Vaults to Preserve the Wines

it dimmed the flames of our torches.

At the farthest end of this crypt was another, even smaller crypt. On three sides, its walls were lined with human remains, piled to the ceiling overhead. But on the fourth wall, the bones, which had been piled high, were now thrown down. They lay in a mound upon the earthen floor. In this wall, we could see still another alcove or recess. It was about four feet deep, three feet wide, and six or seven feet high. It seemed to have been made, not for any special use itself, but as the space between two of the huge pillars supporting the roof of the catacombs.

This alcove was backed by the same thick solid granite wall that surrounded all of these underground rooms. On the surface of this granite wall were imbedded two iron staples, U-shaped pieces of metal, about two feet apart. From one of them hung a long iron chain, with wrist locks at either end.

Fortunato lifted his dull torch, attempting

The Burial Crypt

to see into the depths of this alcove. But his efforts were in vain, because there was no sufficient light.

"Here," I said, "over here is the Amontillado. As for Luchesi . . . ."

"He is an ignoramus," interrupted my friend, stepping forward unsteadily.

I followed immediately at his heels. It took only an instant for him to reach the far wall of the alcove. There, he found his progress halted by the rock wall. He stood stupidly bewildered.

It took me only a second to grasp the chain hanging from one staple, and only a few seconds more to pull it across his waist and lock his wrists in it. He was much too drunk and much too astonished to resist. In a moment, I had him chained to the granite.

I turned the key in each wrist lock, withdrew it, then I stepped back.

"Pass your hand over the wall," I said. "You surely feel the dampness. Once more, let me

Chained to the Granite

*implore* you to return .... No? Then I must positively leave you. But first I must give you all the little attentions in my power."

"The Amontillado!" exclaimed my friend, not yet recovered from his astonishment.

"True," I replied. "The Amontillado."

As I said these words, I busied myself among the pile of bones of which I have already spoken. Throwing them aside, I soon uncovered a pile of building stones and cement I had placed there earlier. With these materials and with the aid of a small trowel I had hidden under my long jacket, I began energetically to wall up the entrance of the alcove.

I had scarcely put down the first layer of building stones when I realized that Fortunato's drunken state was wearing off. I heard a low moaning cry—definitely *not* the cry of a drunken man. Then there was a long, stubborn silence. I laid the second layer of stones ... and the third ... and the fourth.

Walling Up the Entrance to the Alcove

Then I heard the furious clanking of the chain. The noise lasted for several minutes. In order to listen to it with greater satisfaction, I stopped my work and sat down upon the bones.

When at last the clanking stopped, I began my work again, and without further interruption laid the fifth, the sixth, and the seventh layers of stones. The wall was now nearly level with my breast. I stopped again and held the torch over the partially completed wall to throw its light on the figure inside the alcove.

Loud, shrill screams suddenly burst from the throat of the chained form. For an instant I hesitated—I trembled. Could he be heard? But after a moment's thought, I was reassured. I placed my hand upon the solid granite wall and was satisfied.

Fortunato screamed again and again and again, without stopping. I screamed too, re-echoing his shouts. Mine surpassed his in

The Seventh Layer of Stones

volume and in strength. After I did this, the screamer became still.

I completed the eighth, the ninth, and the tenth layers. It was now midnight, and my task was drawing to a close. I had finished a portion of the eleventh and last layer. There remained but a single stone to be fitted and plastered in. I struggled with its weight as I placed it partially in position.

But then from the alcove there came a low laugh that made the hairs stand erect upon my head. The laugh was followed by a sad, quiet voice, which I had difficulty in recognizing as the voice of the noble, haughty Fortunato.

"Ha! ha! ha!—he! he!—a very good joke indeed—an excellent jest," whispered the voice. "We will have many a rich laugh about this—he! he!—over our wine—he! he! he!"

"The Amontillado!" I said.

"He! he! he!—yes, the Amontillado. But it is getting late, is it not? They will all be waiting for us—my Lady Fortunato and the others.

A Single Stone to Be Fitted In

Let us be gone."

"Yes," I said, "let us be gone."

*"For the love of God, Montresor!"*

"Yes," I said, "for the love of God!"

But I listened in vain for a reply to these words. I grew impatient. I called aloud, "Fortunato!"

No answer.

I called again, "Fortunato!"

No answer still. I pushed one of the torches through the remaining opening and let it fall inside the alcove.

From within there came only a jingling of bells.

My heart grew sick—because of the dampness of the catacombs. I hastened to complete my work. I forced the last stone into position and plastered it up. Against the new wall I rebuilt the old pile of bones.

For half of a century now no mortal has disturbed them. *In pace requiescat!* Let him rest in peace!

Let Him Rest in Peace!

# The Fall of the House of Usher

The House of Usher

# The Fall of the House of Usher

One dull, dark day in autumn, I was traveling on horseback through a dreary stretch of countryside. At nightfall, I came in sight of the House of Usher.

This was the home of Roderick Usher, who had been my childhood friend. It had been many years since he and I had seen each other. I lived at the time in a distant part of the country. However, he had recently written me a long letter telling me of a serious illness and of a mental disturbance that had taken hold of him. He said he had to see me, as his best, oldest, and *only* friend. He hoped that his health would improve with my cheerful company. The only answer I could possibly give was to go at once to his home.

Roderick Usher had always been a quiet person who talked little of himself. So I didn't know too much about him. Yet I did know that his family was an old one. Many of his ancestors had been famous for their artistic and musical abilities; others were known for their exceptional generosity and charity. In the part of the country where he lived, the "House of Usher" had come to mean both the family and its ancestral mansion.

Now, on this dark autumn evening, I was approaching the House of Usher. It was a melancholy-looking building, and I looked on it with an icy sinking of the heart. The walls were gray and bleak, covered only by a string-like web of moss and other clinging plants. I looked at the vacant eyelike windows and at the few white bare trunks of decaying trees that still stood in the damp, swampy ground

Traveling Through a Dreary Countryside

surrounding the old house.

As I looked at the house, it seemed to me that it was being wrapped in a strange vaporous cloud. A mystic fog seemed to rise from the decaying trees and nearby swamp until it covered the gray stone walls. Yet the walls stood upright and perfect. Only a few stones were crumbling. A closer look, however, disclosed the tiniest sliver of a crack, zigzagging its way down from the roof. The crack went right down to the wall's foundation, ending under the damp, swampy earth.

Noticing these things, I went up the short road to the house. A servant met me and took my horse, and I entered an arched hallway. Another servant led me to my friend.

We walked silently through many dark and winding passages. I noticed carved ceilings, gloomy tapestries on the walls, and black wooden floors. On a staircase I met the family physician, who introduced himself to me. He hesitated strangely, looking somewhat evil

A Crack Zigzags Down from the Roof.

while at the same time frightened, then continued on his way.

At last the servant threw open a door, and I saw my friend resting in a chair. Roderick Usher rose to greet me with great warmth.

We were in a huge room. The ceiling was high over my head. The windows, long and narrow and pointed, were so high they could be reached only by ladder. Dark draperies covered the walls. The furniture was antique, but tattered and uninteresting. Many books and musical instruments lay scattered about the room, but they gave it no warmth or feeling of life. I seemed to be breathing an atmosphere of great sorrow.

Surely no man had ever changed so greatly in a few years as had Roderick Usher! He had always been thin, with a pale narrow face and large eyes. But now his face was ghostly, his eyes too bright. His silken hair had grown and had not been trimmed. So it now floated wildly about his face, making it look even thinner.

Roderick Usher

He began to talk about his illness. He said it ran in his family—a nervous ailment with many strange and contradictory symptoms, but no cure. His body was so extremely sensitive that only the softest clothing could touch his skin, only the blandest food could tempt him, and only the faintest light could glow without injuring his eyes. He could not bear the odor of any flower, and he was filled with horror by all sounds except the gentlest music played by stringed instruments.

He was also plagued by strange terrors. "I dread the future," he said. "I shudder at the thought of any coming event. I feel that I will lose my life and reason together in some uncanny struggle with a grim fantasy. I know that fantasy to be *fear*."

He talked on, telling me also some superstitions about his mansion that filled him with terror. He could not describe them, other than to say that the gloomy *forms* of the walls and turrets and swamps seemed to be affecting his

Usher Describes His Illness.

*spirit.* Yet for some unexplained reason, he had not been able to bring himself to leave his ancestral home for many years.

Then he went on to explain that his gloomy spirit was further burdened by the severe and incurable illness of his beloved sister, Madeline. She was his sole companion and his last and only relative on earth. "Her death," he said bitterly, "would leave me the last of the ancient family of the Ushers."

While he spoke, Madeline entered through one door at the far end of the room and disappeared through another, without even noticing my presence. I stared at her in astonishment and dread, though I knew not why. When I turned back to her brother, I saw his face buried in his hands and passionate tears trickling through his emaciated fingers.

Madeline's illness, he informed me, quite puzzled her physicians. She had lost interest in everything; she was wasting away to a shadow; and for long periods of time she would

Madeline Enters.

sit or stand quite still, unmoving for hours.

Later that evening, my friend sadly informed me that Madeline had been bedridden with exhaustion and with the deterioration and emaciation caused by her disease. Therefore, the glimpse I had gotten of her would probably be the last I would get, at least while she was living.

After telling me these things, Roderick Usher talked no more of his sister. In the next few days, I tried earnestly to cheer my friend. We read together. Or I listened to his wild strumming on the guitar, his fingers causing it to speak in an unearthly voice.

Usher had also inherited the artistic talents of his ancestors. I watched as he painted. He worked feverishly, painting several canvases in succession. One of his paintings in particular stays in my mind. It was a small picture, showing only the inside of a very long rectangular tunnel, with low walls, smooth and white. The design showed this tunnel to be

Wild Strumming on the Guitar

far below the surface of the earth. There was no window, no opening, no torch to produce any source of light. Yet the scene seemed as bright as though it were lit by the rays of a splendid, hidden sun. How strange!

We talked during those days of many things. Usher confided to me an idea he had, an idea that *things*—even plants and stones—had knowledge and a purpose for being, just as animal and human life has. I was sure that these ideas were proof of his disordered mind . . . until I heard his next statement.

"The proof, dear friend, the proof of what I have said is this. You have seen the swamp that surrounds the walls. There is a cloud—an *atmosphere*—rising from this swamp, swirling about the house. It enfolds the walls, pressing in upon them."

I looked up with a start—for this was the very thought that had overcome me when I approached the old mansion.

Roderick continued, "This *atmosphere* rises

A Strange Painting of a Tunnel

from the swamp to press on me. Thus it influences, shapes, and molds me and my life, just as it has molded the destinies of my family through the ages."

I heard these words with a shudder, and I was glad when my friend got off this subject and turned again to his books.

So the days passed. One evening, my friend informed me that his sister Madeline was no more.

"My dear friend, I am terribly sorry to hear this," I began. But he interrupted my condolences as though he had not heard.

"I intend," he said, "to preserve her body for two weeks before burial. The physicians have been too curious about her strange illness, and they might wish to make further examinations. I fear they might get to her body if we put her into her grave now. But if we wait a while, they will not know when or where we will bury her."

"And where do you plan to do that, my

"I Intend to Preserve Her Body."

friend?" I asked.

"The family burial grounds are quite far away, but there are compartments within the thick stone walls of this house . . . ." His voice trailed off, and he was lost in thought.

An unusual decision, I thought. But if that evil-looking physician I passed on my arrival was one who might disturb Madeline's rest, then Roderick's precaution was wise.

When Madeline's body had been placed in a coffin, Usher and I alone carried it to its temporary tomb. This was a vault, or compartment, in the foundation walls of the mansion. It was small, damp, and without any light. It was directly under the room in which I was staying.

In ancient times it had served as a dungeon. Centuries later it was used to store gunpowder, and the walls, floor, and even the heavy iron door were covered with sheets of copper to keep out the dampness. I noticed particularly the sharp, grating sound made by

We Carry Madeline's Coffin to Its Tomb.

this door as it moved slowly upon its hinges.

We placed our mournful burden upon wooden stands inside this vault. The coffin lid was not yet fastened, and we opened it to look once more on the face of Madeline Usher.

For the first time I noticed the striking resemblance between the brother and sister. My friend, perhaps guessing my thoughts, murmured something about their having been twins. He said that strange understandings had always existed between them—secret understandings unknown to anyone else.

But we couldn't bear to look upon her for long. Her illness had left a faint redness on her face and a suspiciously lingering smile on her lips—a smile which is terrible in death. We replaced the coffin lid and screwed it down. Then we left the vault, fastening the iron door behind us, and went upstairs into the upper portion of the house. This was almost as gloomy as the vault we had just left.

As the days passed, a change came over my

One Last Look at Madeline Usher

grieving friend. No more did he play his guitar, paint, or even read. Instead, he roamed constantly from room to room, with hurried but purposeless steps. His face became, if possible, even more pale and ghastly. His once-bright eyes became dull.

He spoke with a nervous tremor which seemed to come from some unknown terror. There were times I thought he struggled for the courage to confide to me a terrible secret. Then the moment would pass. At other times, I became convinced it was his madness, for he stared into space for hours. He seemed to be listening to some imaginary sound.

His condition terrified me—and then it infected me. I felt myself coming under the spell of the nameless terrors and the superstitions that so profoundly affected him.

This feeling grew upon me gradually. It reached its full power about a week after we had placed the lady Madeline in the dungeon.

It was a stormy night. I could not sleep. I

Usher Stares into Space for Hours.

lay awake as the dark hours passed. I tried to use my reason to get rid of the nervousness that came over me. I tried to tell myself that the gloomy furniture of my room and the dark draperies—they must be the cause of the oppressive feeling that lay upon me.

But the terror would not leave me. Instead, it seemed to settle on me more heavily. I tried again to rid myself of its weight. I sat up in bed and listened to the sounds of the night. Through the storm I heard strange low, faint sounds. Then they ceased, only to begin again after a few minutes. I was overcome by a strong sense of horror.

I knew I would sleep no more that night, so I rose and hastily dressed. I tried now to get rid of the dread feelings by pacing the floor.

I had taken only a few turns in this manner when I heard a step in the corridor. In an instant, Usher was rapping at my door. He stared about the room silently for some minutes. Then he spoke.

Unable to Sleep

"You have not seen it?" he asked. "You have not—but you shall!" With that, he hurried to a window and opened it to the storm.

A furious gust of wind entered and nearly lifted us from our feet. It was a tempestuous yet strangely beautiful night. Clouds hung thickly about the turreted roof of the house. The wind blew in violent gusts, pausing now and again. The clouds were tossed about, coming together and then being blown apart before our eyes. The lower surfaces of the moving clouds and the tree trunks all about the house were bathed in an eerie glow. Yet no moon shone; no stars twinkled; no lightning flashed. What then was this strange, unnatural light that seemed to be circling about the old mansion?

"You must not—you shall not watch this!" I said with a shudder to Usher. I led him firmly away from the window to a chair. "These wild visions—they are simply electrical

Usher Opens the Window to the Storm.

phenomena. From the storm. Or perhaps they rise from the swamp. I'll close the window— the air is too chilly and damp for you."

I did so, and he did not protest. "Now," I said, picking up the nearest book, "I will read to you, and so we'll pass this stormy night."

The story was an old adventure tale. The hero, Ethelred, set out to do battle with an evil hermit. I read, "Arriving at the hermit's door, Ethelred lifted his sword and struck several blows in the wooden planks, cracking and ripping them apart."

As I finished that sentence, my breath suddenly caught in my throat . . . I paused. It seemed to me (or was it my imagination?) that from some remote part of the house came an exact sound like the one I had just described— a cracking and ripping of wood!

Probably the storm, I thought, and returned to the story. "Inside the house, there was no sign of the hermit. Instead, Ethelred saw before him a scaly dragon with a tongue of fire.

Reading to Pass the Stormy Night

The dragon was sitting guard before a palace of gold, with a floor made of silver. And Ethelred uplifted his sword and struck off the head of the dragon. As it fell, the beast gave forth a horrible and piercing shriek . . . . ''

At these words, there came to my ears a low and distant cry. It was a screaming or grating sound, very like the dragon's shriek of which I had just read. But this cry was *not* my imagination. I *did* hear it.

The nameless terror I had felt in my sleepless bed earlier in the evening came over me again. But I was concerned for the nervous state of my friend, and I tried not to excite him. Perhaps he had not heard the distant cry. Perhaps I had imagined it?

But a strange change had come over him. We had been sitting facing each other, but now he turned his chair away from me and faced it toward the door. His lips were trembling; his head was dropped on his chest; and his eyes were open wide. In this position,

Hearing a Distant Shriek

he began swaying from side to side.

To take his attention away from whatever he might have heard, I began hastily to read again.

"And now Ethelred pulled the dragon's body out of the way. Bravely he approached the castle, walking on the silver pavement.

"Over the castle doorway hung an enchanted shield of brass—the prize for anyone brave enough to kill the dragon. As Ethelred approached, the shield fell down at his feet upon the silver floor, with a mighty, great, and terrible ringing sound."

No sooner had these words passed my lips than I became aware of another sound. It was a distant, hollow, metallic sound. Completely unnerved, I leaped to my feet. But Usher seemed undisturbed. He was still swaying gently from side to side, his eyes staring at nothing.

I rushed to him and placed my hand on his shoulder to soothe him. A shudder came over

I Try to Soothe Usher.

his entire body, and he began to speak in a low hurried murmur, unaware that I was ever there.

"Not hear it?—yes, I hear it, and *have* heard it," he said through quivering lips. "Long—long—long—many minutes, many hours, many days, have I heard it. Yet I dared not—oh pity me, miserable wretch that I am!—*I dared not speak! We have put her living in the tomb!* I told you how sensitive I have become in my illness! Many days ago, I heard her first feeble movements in the coffin—*yet I dared not speak!* And now—tonight—Ethelred—the breaking of the hermit's door—the death-cry of the dragon—the clanging of the brass shield as it fell—what they really were, were the breaking of her coffin lid, the grating of the iron door of her prison, and her struggling to get out of the copper vault. Oh! Where can I fly? She will be here soon to punish me for burying her before she was dead! Even now I hear her footstep on the stair! Even now I hear

"We Have Put Her Living in the Tomb!"

the horrible beating of her heart!"

At this, he sprang furiously to his feet.

"Madman!" he shrieked. *"Madman! I tell you that she now stands outside this door!"*

At his last words, the huge antique door opened slowly. From what? From a rushing gust of wind? . . .And there, standing in the doorway, was the shrouded figure of the lady Madeline of Usher. There was blood upon her white robes, and the evidence of a bitter struggle was upon every inch of her body.

For a moment she stood trembling in the doorway. Then, with a low moaning cry, she flew to her brother and threw herself violently upon him. With a cry of final death-agony, she dragged him with her to the floor—a corpse. Roderick Usher was dead, a victim of the terrors he, himself, had foreseen.

In my own terror, I fled from that room and from that mansion.

The storm was still raging as I found myself out on the road.

Madeline Drags Usher to the Floor.

Suddenly, a wild light flashed across the path in front of me. I turned to see where it came from, for behind me were only the vast house and its shadows.

Then I saw where the strange light was coming from—it was the blood-red light of a full, setting moon. It glowed through a crack in the wall of the house—the same zigzag crack I had noticed on my arrival—the crack that zigzagged its way down from the roof to end in the damp, swampy earth.

While I gazed, this crack rapidly widened. Suddenly, a fierce gust of wind—a whirlwind—burst upon the house.

My brain reeled as I saw the once-mighty walls come crashing down. I heard a tumultuous shouting, like the roaring voice of a thousand oceans. I stood there frozen, gazing in awe, as the tumbling walls began to sink. Then the deep swamp at my feet closed angrily and silently over the fragments of the "House of Usher."

The Once-Mighty Walls Come Crashing Down.

# The Gold-Bug

William Legrand and His Companion, Jupiter

# The Gold-Bug

## PART 1

## In the Warmth of the Fire

After a series of misfortunes reduced his once-wealthy family to near-poverty, William Legrand left his native city of New Orleans, Louisiana. He was depressed and discouraged, too ashamed of his misfortunes to face old friends.

With one companion, Legrand came to live on Sullivan's Island, near Charleston, South Carolina. His single companion was Jupiter, an elderly slave who had been given his freedom before the loss of the family fortune. Because of his concern for his former master and because he was too old to enter a new occupation, Jupiter had decided to accompany Legrand and look after him.

Sullivan's Island is about three miles long and a quarter of a mile wide. A narrow creek oozes its way through weeds and slime along one long side and separates the island from the South Carolina mainland. The opposite side of the island faces the sea. Because the island is almost all sand, there are few trees or plants. At the western end of the island is Fort Moultrie, and here, amid several small summer cottages, stand a few clusters of the bristly palmetto, a small palm tree with fan-shaped leaves. The rest of the island is covered with sweet myrtle, a shrub which fills the air with its fragrance and manages somehow to grow quite thick and quite tall, sometimes fifteen or twenty feet.

Legrand and Jupiter had built a small hut in the midst of this tall thick shrubbery at the eastern end of the island. I was living in Charleston at the time, but my love of nature

Sullivan's Island

often took me across the creek to the island. Although Legrand was called by some a hermit, we had met during one of my visits and became friends. He had an unusually keen mind and was very well educated. He was, though, a strangely moody person who could jump with enthusiasm at one moment and become silent and melancholy the next. This was due, I always supposed, to the changes in his family's fortune. But he seemed to look forward to my occasional visits to his hut, and I enjoyed his company.

Others might have thought his existence an isolated one, but Legrand actually kept quite busy. His chief amusements were hunting and fishing, or walking along the beach and through the myrtles, searching for shells and insect specimens. He had quite a fine collection of both and was very knowledgeable about entomology, the study of insect life.

One October day a few years ago—1840, I think it was—I decided to visit my friend

Legrand Searches for Shells.

whom I had not seen in several weeks. Usually the weather on Sullivan's Island is quite mild, even in the winter. In the autumn, it is seldom necessary to light a fire, but this day was quite chilly.

Just before sunset I reached the hut. I rapped, as I usually did, but there was no reply. I knew where the key was hidden, so I unlocked the door and went in.

A fine fire was blazing upon the hearth, a most welcome sight, although an unusual one here. I sat down gratefully in an armchair near the crackling logs, and in a little while my hosts arrived.

They greeted me cordially, and Jupiter, grinning from ear to ear, bustled about to prepare supper. Legrand was in one of his moods of enthusiasm. He had found a new king of shell and, even more exciting, a scarab—a kind of black winged beetle, once considered sacred by the ancient Egyptians.

"I believe this scarab to be totally new,

I Reach the Hut.

never described by any scientist before," he shouted joyfully. "And I hope to have your opinion about it tomorrow."

"And why not tonight?" I inquired, rubbing my hands over the blaze.

"Ah, if I only knew you were coming!" answered Legrand. "But it's been so long since I've seen you. How could I have guessed that you would visit this very night? On the way home I met Lieutenant Gray from Fort Moultrie. You know how interested he is in natural science. Foolishly, I lent him the bug. So it will be impossible for you to see it until morning. Stay here tonight, and I will send Jupe for it at sunrise. It is the loveliest thing in creation!"

"What is the loveliest—the sunrise?"

"No, the bug, of course. It's a brilliant gold color, about the size of a large hickory nut. It has two jet black spots at one end of its back and a single long black spot at the other end. The antennae are . . . ."

Legrand Talks About the Bug.

"It's a gole-bug, Mister Will," cut in Jupiter, "solid gole, every bit of him, inside and all, 'cept the wing. I never felt such a heavy bug in my life!"

"Well, suppose it is, Jupe," returned Legrand, "is that any reason for letting our dinner burn? The color . . ." here he turned to me, " . . . the color is really close to Jupiter's description. The scales have the most brilliant metallic shine! You'll see for yourself tomorrow. In the meantime, this will give you some idea of the shape."

Saying this, he sat down at a small table. On it were pen and ink, but no paper. He hunted in his pockets until he found what looked like a scrap of dirty note paper.

"Never mind," he said. "I'll use this." And on the note paper he made a rough drawing with his pen. When he had finished sketching, he handed it to me without rising.

I returned to my seat by the fire, for I was still chilled after my long walk. As I took the

Legrand Sketches the Bug.

drawing, I heard a loud growl and the sound of scratching at the door. Jupiter went to open it, and a large dog rushed in. This was Wolf, Legrand's Newfoundland, to whom I had given much attention on my earlier visits. The dog now leaped upon my shoulders and loaded me with caresses.

After Wolf and I had frolicked a bit, I turned my attention to Legrand's drawing. To tell the truth, I was quite puzzled at what I saw.

"Well!" I exclaimed after studying the paper for some minutes. "This *is* a strange scarab, I agree. I never saw anything like it before—unless it was a death's-head — a skull. That's what it looks most like to me."

"A death's-head!" repeated Legrand in surprise. "Oh—yes—well, I guess it does look something like that on paper. The two upper black spots look like eyes, eh? And the longer one at the bottom like a mouth—and then the shape of the whole is oval."

"Perhaps so," I said. "But, Legrand, I can

Wolf Frolics with Me.

see you are not an artist. I'll just have to wait to see the beetle itself."

"Not an artist?" he repeated. "I always thought I could draw fairly well." He was clearly offended. "I had some good teachers at one time."

"But you must be joking then," I said. "This is a very fine drawing of a *skull*. Your beetle must be the queerest scarab in the world to resemble it. But where are the antennae you spoke of?"

"The antennae!" Legrand was all but shouting now. "You *must* see the antennae. I drew them quite distinctly."

"Perhaps so," I said as soothingly as I could. "Perhaps you have, but I still don't see them."

Without further comment, I handed him the paper. I was quite surprised at his change of mood. And as for his drawing of the beetle, there were positively *no antennae*, and the thing *did* look very like . . . a death's-head.

The Scarab Looks Like a Skull.

He took the paper with a look of annoyance and was about to crumple it up and throw it into the fire, when a quick glance at the design seemed to startle him. His face grew red. Then he turned quite pale. Sitting quite still at the table, he studied the drawing carefully.

Then he stood up and, taking a candle from the table, went to sit upon a sea-chest in the farthest corner of the room. Here again he studied the paper carefully, turning it in all directions. However, he didn't say a word.

I was quite amazed at his behavior, but thought it best not to risk irritating him any further. So I remained silent also.

Presently he took a wallet from his pocket and placed the paper carefully in it. He unlocked a writing-desk and placed the wallet inside, locking it again. Now he grew calmer. But the enthusiasm he had shown earlier in the evening was gone.

As the evening wore on, he became more and more absorbed in his own thoughts, and no

Legrand Studies the Drawing.

conversation of mine could rouse him. I had planned to spend the night at the hut, as I had often done before. But because of Legrand's mood, I decided to leave. He did not insist on my staying, but as I left, he shook my hand with what seemed to me to be a highly emotional grip.

For the next month I did not see Legrand. Then one day, Jupiter appeared at my home in Charleston. He looked so downcast that I feared some serious disaster had occurred.

"Welcome, Jupe," I said. "But what is the matter? How is Mister Will?"

"To tell the truth, sir, he's not too well. Not too well at all."

"Not well! I'm sorry to hear it. What does he complain of?"

"There—that's it!" exclaimed Jupiter. "He never complains of a thing, but I can tell he's very sick."

"*Very* sick, Jupiter? Why didn't you say so at once?"

Jupiter Appears at My Home.

"Why, sir, it's nothing to get excited about. Mister Will says nothing's the matter with him. But then—why does he walk about with his head down and his shoulders up and his face as white as a ghost?"

"Jupiter, haven't you any idea of what is causing this? Has anything unpleasant happened since I saw you?"

"No, sir, hasn't been anything unpleasant *since* then. It was *before* then—it was the very day you were there."

"How? What do you mean?"

"Why, sir, I mean the bug—the gole-bug he found. I never did see such a devilish bug. It kicked and bit everything that came near it. Mister Will caught it first, but he had to let it go again mighty quick. I tell you, that was when he must have got bitten. I didn't like the look of the bug's mouth myself, to tell the truth, so I wouldn't grab him with my fingers. Instead, I caught hold of him with a piece of paper that I found. I wrapped him up in the

Jupiter Grabbed the Bug with Paper.

paper and stuffed a piece of it in his mouth."

"And you really think that Mister Will was bitten by the beetle and that the bite made him sick?"

"I don't think nothin' about it—I *know* it," Jupiter answered emphatically. "Why else do he dream about gole so much, if it ain't because he was bit by the gole-bug? I've heard about gole-bugs before."

"How do you know he dreams about gold?"

"How? Because he talks about it in his sleep—that's how!"

"Well, Jupe, perhaps you are right. But about your coming here today—did you bring any message for me?"

"Not a message, sir. I brought this letter." And here, Jupiter handed me this note:

MY DEAR FRIEND,

SINCE I SAW YOU, I HAVE HAD GREAT CAUSE FOR ANXIETY. I HAVE SOMETHING TO TELL YOU, YET I DON'T KNOW HOW TO TELL IT OR EVEN WHETHER I SHOULD TELL IT AT ALL.

"I Brought This Letter."

I HAVE NOT BEEN QUITE WELL FOR SOME DAYS PAST, AND I KNOW POOR OLD JUPE WORRIES ABOUT ME.

I HAVE NOT FOUND ANYTHING NEW FOR MY COLLECTION SINCE YOU WERE HERE.

IF YOU POSSIBLY CAN, COME BACK WITH JUPITER. DO COME. I WISH TO SEE YOU TONIGHT, UPON BUSINESS OF THE HIGHEST IMPORTANCE.

> EVER YOURS,
> WILLIAM LEGRAND

The tone of this note made me very uneasy. It was so different from Legrand's usual style. What "business of the highest importance" could he possibly have with me? Jupiter's description of his condition worried me too. I was afraid that his misfortunes had finally unsettled his sanity. Without a moment's hesitation, therefore, I prepared to go back to the island with Jupiter. I agreed to meet him at the wharf in a short while.

A scythe and three spades, all new, were

The Note Makes Me Uneasy.

lying in the bottom of the boat when I reached the wharf. "What are these for, Jupiter?" I asked.

"Mister Will insisted I buy them in the town. And a lot of money I had to pay for them too."

"But what is he going to do with them?"

"That's more than I know," Jupiter replied. "But it's all because of that bug."

It was clear that I was not going to get any information or satisfaction from Jupiter, for his mind seemed completely absorbed by the bug. So I stepped into the boat, and we set sail. With a strong breeze we soon landed just north of Fort Moultrie on Sullivan's Island. A walk of some two miles brought us to the hut at about three in the afternoon. Legrand was eagerly waiting for us.

Setting Sail for the Island

Legrand Grasps My Hand Nervously.

# The Gold-Bug

## PART 2

## Beetle on a String

Legrand grasped my hand nervously. His face was pale, and his deep-set eyes seemed unusually bright, even glaring. Seeing his ghastly appearance, I shared Jupiter's concern about his health. But when I asked about it, Legrand brushed aside my questions. Not knowing what else to say, I asked if he had gotten the beetle back yet from Lieutenant Gray.

"Oh, yes," he replied, and his face reddened. "I got it from him the next morning. Nothing will tempt me to part with that scarab ever again. Do you know that Jupiter is quite right about it?"

"How do you mean?" I asked, alarmed.

"In saying it's *real gold*." He said this in such a serious tone that I was truly shocked.

"This bug will make my fortune," he continued mysteriously, smiling in triumph. "It will restore my family possessions. Is it any wonder that I prize it? Since Fortune has seen fit to give it to me, I must use it properly, and then I shall find the gold. For the gold-bug is the key to it."

At this, Legrand rose, took the beetle from a glass case, and brought it to me. It was indeed a beautiful scarab and, at that time, of a variety unknown to naturalists. Of course, it was a great prize from a scientific point of view. There were two round black spots near one end of the back and a long black spot near the other end, just as he had described. The scales were hard and glossy, with all the appearance of polished gold.

The weight of the insect was remarkable too,

The Scarab Is *Real Gold*.

and taking all things into consideration, I could hardly blame Jupiter for believing it was solid gold. But what was I to make of Legrand's agreeing with him? Surely, even an amateur scientist would know better!

"I sent for you," Legrand began dramatically, in a strange booming voice, "to have your advice concerning Fate and the bug and . . . ."

"My dear Legrand," I interrupted, "you are certainly ill and had better go to bed. I will stay with you a few days until you get over this. You are feverish and . . . ."

"Feel my pulse," he said, now back to his usual voice.

I felt his pulse and, to tell the truth, found not the slightest indication of fever. "But you may be ill and yet have no fever. First, go to bed. Then . . . ."

"You are mistaken," he broke in. "I am as well as I can be under the circumstances. It is only the excitement which I feel. If you really

144

"Feel My Pulse."

want to help me, you will share this excitement."

"And how can I do that?"

"Very easily. Jupiter and I are going on an expedition into the hills on the mainland. We shall need help. You are the only one we can trust. It doesn't matter whether we succeed or fail. Either way, my excitement will be satisfied and I will rest easy."

"I would do anything to help you," I replied, "but do you mean to say that this infernal beetle has something to do with your expedition into the hills?"

"It has."

"Then, Legrand, I cannot become a party to such an absurd expedition."

"But it will only be for one night," he protested. "We shall start immediately and be back by sunrise."

"And will you promise me, upon your honor, that when this madness of yours is over and the bug business settled, you will then return

Legrand Pleads with Me.

home and follow my advice until you recover?"

"Yes, yes, I promise. Now let's be off. We have no time to lose."

With a heavy heart, I accompanied my friend. We started at about four o'clock in the afternoon—Legrand, Jupiter, the dog, and myself. Jupiter insisted on carrying the scythe and the spades—more because he feared to trust Legrand with them than out of any zeal for hard work.

I carried a couple of lanterns, while Legrand contented himself with carrying the scarab which was attached to the end of a long length of cord. He twirled it to and fro as he walked, with the air of a sorcerer. I thought this was surely evidence of his loss of sanity, and I was terribly upset. But I didn't want to disturb his mind any more than it already was, so I reluctantly continued along in silence.

We crossed the creek separating Sullivan's Island from the mainland in a small boat. Once ashore, we started climbing the high grounds.

Legrand Twirls the Scarab as He Walks.

going in a northwesterly direction through a desolate stretch of countryside. No trace of a human footstep was to be seen. Legrand led the way, pausing only here and there to check out certain landmarks.

After about two hours, when the sun was just setting, we entered an even drearier landscape. This was a flat region near the top of a heavily wooded hill. The thickly overgrown bramble bushes grew in between huge rocks on the hill. We had climbed onto a sort of natural platform, with Jupiter cutting our way through with the scythe, until we came to an enormously tall tulip tree, surrounded by eight or ten short oaks.

Never did I see so tall a tree, nor one so beautiful in its foliage and form, in the wide spread of its branches, and in the general majesty of its appearance.

Legrand turned to Jupiter. "Jupe, do you think you can climb it?" he asked.

The old man seemed a little staggered by the

An Enormous Tulip Tree

question. He walked slowly around the thick trunk and examined it closely.

"Yes, Mister Will, I can climb any tree I ever saw in my life."

"Then up with you as soon as possible. It will soon be too dark to see what we must see."

"How far up must I go?"

"Get up the main trunk first and then I will tell you what to do. Here, wait! Take the beetle with you."

"The bug, Mister Will? The gole-bug? What must I take that thing for?"

"Jupe, if you are afraid—a great big fellow like you—to carry a harmless little dead beetle, why then you can hold it by this string. But if you do not take it up with you in some way, I shall have to break your head with this shovel!"

"I was just joking!" exclaimed Jupiter. "What do I care about an ole bug?" And saying this, he cautiously took hold of the end of the string and, keeping the insect as far

"How Far Up Must I Go?"

from his body as possible, started up the tree.

Young tulip trees have peculiarly smooth trunks. They often grow to a great height before their branches develop. At a riper age the bark becomes gnarled and uneven, and many short limbs branch off from the main trunk. Thus, it was not really difficult for Jupiter to get a footing, since the trunk, tall as it was, was a natural ladder.

Jupiter reached the first large branch, some sixty or seventy feet from the ground, in short order. Wriggling himself into the fork of the branch and the trunk, he seemed to consider his mission accomplished.

"What now, Mister Will?" he called down.

"Follow up the largest branch—the one on this side," called back Legrand.

Jupiter obeyed him promptly and apparently with little trouble. He climbed higher and higher until we could no longer see his squat figure through the thick foliage surrounding him. Presently we heard his

Jupiter Reaches the First Large Branch.

voice.

"How much farther?" he called down.

"How high are you?" asked Legrand.

"I can see the sky through the top."

"Never mind the sky," called back Legrand. "Listen carefully. Look *down* the trunk. Coun the branches below you on this side. Ho many are there?"

"One, two, three, four, five—five big ones o this side."

"Then go one branch higher."

In a few minutes Jupiter's voice was hear again, announcing that he was now on th seventh branch.

"Now, Jupe," called Legrand excitedly, " want you to work your way out upon tha branch as far as you can. If you see anythin strange, let me know."

By this time, I was certain of my poo friend's insanity, and I became anxious abou getting him home.

"'Most out to the end now." Jupiter'

"How High Are You?"

distant voice interrupted my thoughts.

"Out to the end!" screamed Legrand. "Are you out to the end yet?"

"Soon be out to the end, Mister Will. O-o-o-o-h! Lord-God-Awmighty! What is this here on the tree?"

"Well, what is it?" shouted back Legrand, suddenly seeming quite delighted.

"Why, 'taint nothing but a skull—somebody left his head up in the tree, that's all. And the crows gobbled off every bit of the meat."

"A skull, you say! Now tell me, how is it fastened to the branch? What holds it on?"

"Just a minute now—let me look. Why, that's very strange—there's a big nail in the skull, holding it on to the tree."

"Now, Jupiter, can you hear me? Do exactly as I tell you."

"Yes, Mister Will."

"Pay attention, then. Find the left eye—*the left eye* of the skull. Do you know your right hand from your left?"

"Why, 'Taint Nothing But a Skull."

"Yes. It's my left hand I chop wood with."

"To be sure—you *are* left-handed. And your left eye is on the same side as your left hand. Now find the *left* eye of the skull."

There was a long pause.

"Have you found it yet?" called Legrand anxiously.

"Is the left eye of the skull on the same side as the left hand of the skull? 'Cause the skull ain't got a hand at all! Never mind—here's the left eye! Now what do I do with it?"

"Drop the beetle through it. Let it drop down as far as the string will reach—but don't let go of the string until I tell you."

"All done, Mister Will. It was mighty easy putting the bug through the hole! Watch out for him below!"

As Jupiter spoke, the beetle became visible at the end of the string. It hung quite clear of any branches and glistened like a glob of polished gold in the last rays of the setting sun.

Jupiter Drops the Beetle on a String.

"All right, Jupiter, let it fall!" shouted Legrand. "Careful, now!"

The insect fell like a heavy weight at our feet. Legrand immediately drove a peg into the ground precisely at the spot where the beetle fell.

"Well done, Jupiter. You can come down now!"

While the old man was clambering down, Legrand took a tape measure from his pocket. Fastening one end of it to the tree trunk on the side nearest the peg, he unrolled it until it reached the peg. Then he unrolled it farther in the same direction, continuing in a straight line fifty feet past the peg. There, he drove a second peg into the ground. Using this second peg as a center and the tape measure as a compass, he scratched a circle about four feet in diameter in the dirt. Then Legrand picked up one of the spades and, giving the others to Jupiter and to me, begged us to dig inside this circle as quickly as possible.

Legrand Unrolls the Tape Measure.

To tell the truth, I did not particularly enjoy digging at any time, and at that moment I would have preferred to refuse. Night was coming on. It had been a long day for me. I was already quite tired from the long climb, and I did not look forward to the hike back in pitch darkness. But I saw no way out, and I was afraid it would disturb my poor friend's mental balance if I refused.

It seemed to me that Legrand, in his illness, was believing some Southern superstitions about buried money. And his fantasy had probably been fed by finding the scarab or, perhaps, by Jupiter's idea that it was "a bug of real gold." A mind on the brink of insanity would easily be led by such suggestions. I recalled the poor fellow's speech about the beetle's being "the key to his fortune." I was sadly disturbed about his condition, but I decided that the best thing would be to dig willingly. I would do what I could to hasten the moment when we could convince Legrand,

Beginning to Dig

by finding nothing, that his hopes were in vain.

We lit lanterns and fell to work with a zeal worthy of a more sensible project. We dug steadily, talking little. The only sounds were the thuds of earth as it dropped from our shovels and the yelpings of the dog who took great interest in our activity.

After about two hours, we had reached a depth of five feet, but there was no sign of any treasure. I began to hope that the game was over. Legrand, however, evidently much distressed, insisted that we enlarge the circumference of the circle and dig some more.

Still nothing appeared. Legrand finally climbed out of the pit with the bitterest disappointment on his face. I gladly followed him. Jupiter began to gather up the tools. With Wolf at our heels, we silently turned toward home.

We had taken no more than a dozen steps in this direction when, with a loud oath, Legrand

Climbing out of the Pit, Disappointed!

turned on Jupiter and seized him by the collar.

"You scoundrel!" he hissed from between his clenched teeth. "You infernal villain! Speak, I tell you! Tell me this instant—*Which is your left eye?*"

The astonished fellow opened his eyes and mouth to the fullest, dropped the spades, and trembled on shaky knees.

"Oh, Mister Will! Ain't this here my left eye?" stammered the terrified Jupiter, placing his hand upon his *right* eye.

"I thought so! I knew it!" exclaimed Legrand, letting Jupiter go and jumping about in excitement. "Come, we must go back! There's no time to lose!" And he again led the way to the tulip tree.

"Jupiter, come here!" he ordered when we reached the tree. "Was the skull nailed to the branch with the face outward, or with the face toward the tree?"

"The face was out, Mister Will."

"Well, then," said Legrand, touching each of

*"Which Is Your Left Eye?"*

Jupiter's eyes, "was it *this* eye or *that* through which you dropped the beetle?"

"It was *this* eye, the left one, just as you tole me." And here Jupiter pointed to his *right* eye.

"Good—we must try it again."

Now I thought I saw some method to my friend's madness. He took the peg marking the spot where the beetle first fell and moved it about three inches to the west. Then he fastened the tape measure to the tree trunk and unrolled it again to the peg. As before, he continued it in a straight line to the distance of fifty feet and drove in the second peg. This new spot was several yards away from the point at which we had been digging before.

Here we marked a new circle and again began to dig. I was dreadfully weary, but strangely I no longer felt any distaste for the work. I had become most interested, even, I must admit, excited. I now dug eagerly and found myself looking expectantly for the imagined treasure.

Legrand Marks a New Circle.

When we had been at work perhaps an hour and a half, Wolf suddenly leaped into the hole tearing up the ground frantically with his claws. In a few seconds, he had uncovered a mass of human bones, forming two skeletons. One or two strokes of a spade revealed the blade of a large Spanish knife and, as we dug further, three or four loose pieces of gold coins came to light.

At the sight of these, Jupiter could scarcely contain his joy. Legrand, however, still looked extremely disappointed.

"Come on," he urged us, "keep digging."

The words were hardly out of his mouth when the toe of my boot got caught in something. I stumbled and fell forward into the loose earth.

Scrambling to my feet, I brushed myself off and looked down to see what I had stumbled against. It was a large iron ring, half-buried, rusty, and encrusted with earth.

I Stumble Against a Large Iron Ring.

A Rectangular Wooden Chest Is Unearthed.

# The Gold-Bug

## PART 3

## Links in a Chain

Now we all worked feverishly. Never had I been so excited! In a few minutes, we unearthed a rectangular wooden chest about three and a half feet long, three feet wide, and two and a half feet deep. It was bound around on all sides with straps of rusty iron. On each side of the chest, near the top, were three iron rings, large enough for a hand to grasp, six in all. It was on one of these rings that I had stumbled.

Six men could have carried the chest by means of those rings. And all their strength would have been needed for the task. The chest was so heavy that our combined efforts served only to shift its position very slightly.

We saw at once that it would be impossible to remove so great a weight. Fortunately, the lid was fastened only by two sliding bolts. Trembling and panting with anxiety, we slid back the bolts.

In an instant, a treasure of incalculable value lay gleaming before us! The rays of our lanterns fell onto a confused heap of gold and jewels with a glare that absolutely dazzled our eyes.

Jupiter fell upon his knees in the pit and buried his naked arms up to the elbows in the gold. At length, with a deep sigh, he exclaimed, "And all this came from the gole-bug!"

After much confusion as to what to do next, we decided that we had to remove the treasure before daylight. It would take two trips to get everything from the pit and across to the island. First we removed two-thirds of the

A Treasure Lay Gleaming Before Us.

box's contents so we could raise it from the hole. The articles taken out were left hidden among the bramble bushes, and Wolf was left to guard them, with strict orders from Jupiter not to move or open his mouth until our return. The three of us hastened toward the island with the chest, glad now of the dark night that concealed us.

We reached Legrand's hut safely at one o'clock in the morning. We were too exhausted to start back immediately, so we rested until two o'clock, then had a quick supper and started back for the hills. Luckily, there were three strong sacks in the hut, and we took them with us.

We arrived at the pit a little before four o'clock and found everything as we had left it. We divided the remainder of the treasure as equally as possible among us and again set out for the hut, Wolf at our heels. We reached it and deposited our golden burdens just as the first faint streaks of dawn gleamed from over

Wolf Guards Part of the Treasure.

the tree tops in the East.

We were now thoroughly exhausted, but we were too excited to sleep. After a few hours rest, we all arose to examine our treasure.

The chest had been full to the brim, and it took all that day and the greater part of the night to sort its contents. We found even vaster wealth than we had at first supposed.

There was a great variety of antique gold coins—French, Spanish, German, and English—which we estimated to be worth $150,000. There was, however, no American money. Some of the coins were extremely large and heavy, but so worn that we could not read their inscriptions.

Then there were jewels—large, fine diamonds, a hundred ten in all; eighteen brilliant rubies; three hundred ten emeralds, all very beautiful; twenty-one sapphires; and one opal. These precious stones had all been broken from the gold settings of rings, neckpieces, and pins they had once belonged

A Vast Wealth of Coins and Jewels

to, and had been thrown loose into the chest. When we picked these gold pieces out from among the other gold, we saw that they had been beaten with hammers to prevent anyone's identifying them. That was obviously the reason why the stones had been removed too.

Besides all this, there was a vast quantity of solid gold ornaments—nearly two hundred finger rings and earrings; many rich chains; eighty-three large, heavy crosses; an enormous golden punch bowl, richly ornamented; and many other smaller articles. The weight of these valuables was more than three hundred fifty pounds.

And then there were one hundred ninety-seven superb gold watches, three of them being worth five hundred dollars each. All were very old and, as timekeepers, quite useless, since their works had corroded while they were buried in the damp earth. But all were richly jeweled and set in cases of gold.

A Superb Gold Watch

We estimated that the entire contents of the chest was worth a million and a half dollars. Later, when we sold most of the treasure (keeping a few trinkets and jewels for our own use), we found that we had greatly underestimated its worth.

"Legrand, my dear friend," I kept asking impatiently while we sorted and exclaimed over our find, "how did you know?"

"Later, later," he kept replying.

His pallor and melancholy, I was glad to note, had certainly disappeared, and neither Jupiter nor I were worried any longer about his mental health.

Finally we were done.

"Now you *must* explain," I insisted.

"Very well," said Legrand. "You remember the night I showed you that rough sketch of the beetle? You insisted that it resembled a death's-head. At first, I thought you were making fun of my artistic talent, and I was annoyed at you. So, when you returned the

Legrand Explains How He Knew.

scrap of *parchment* to me, I started to crumple it up and throw it into the fire."

"The scrap of *paper*, you mean?" I asked.

"It *did* look like paper, but when I was drawing on it, I realized it was very thin parchment. It was quite dirty, you remember. Well, just as I was about to crumple it up, I happened to glance at the sketch I had drawn. You can imagine my astonishment when I saw a drawing of a death's-head, but it was not in the place where *I* had drawn the beetle.

"I knew that *my* design was very different—although there *was* a certain similarity in the general outline. If you remember, I took a candle and went to the far end of the room to study the parchment more closely. Then when I turned the parchment over, I saw my own sketch on the *other* side, just as I had made it.

"At first, I was merely surprised at the remarkably similar outlines. It seemed just a strange coincidence that, unknown to me, there was a skull on the other side,

The Skull Was on the *Other* Side.

immediately beneath *my* drawing of the scarab. But gradually I realized something that startled me even more."

"What was that?" I asked, dying with impatience for a solution of this most extraordinary riddle.

"I suddenly remembered that there positively *had not been anything* on the parchment when I first made my drawing. I remembered that I had pulled the scrap from my pocket and turned it first to one side, then to the other to find the cleanest spot. If the skull had been there, of course I would have noticed it.

"I decided to give the matter closer attention later that night, after you left and when Jupiter would be asleep. That is why I did not press you to spend the night, as you planned at first. In the meantime, I locked the parchment safely away in my writing-desk.

"First I considered *how* I had found the parchment. We discovered the beetle on the

Legrand Had Looked on Both Sides.

mainland coast, a short distance above the high-water mark. When I picked it up, the beetle gave me a sharp bite. So I let it drop. Jupiter, who is always cautious, looked about for a leaf or something with which to take hold of it. At this moment, we both spotted the scrap of parchment, which I then thought was paper. It was half-buried in the sand, with only one corner sticking up. Nearby, I noticed the rotting wood of what appeared to have been the hull of a ship's longboat. The wreck must have been there for a very long time.

"Anyway, Jupiter picked up the parchment, wrapped the beetle in it, and gave it to me. On the way home, we met Lieutenant Gray. I showed him the insect, and he asked if he could take it home to study for the evening. When I agreed, he immediately put it into his pocket, *without* the parchment in which it had been wrapped—the parchment which I continued to hold in my hand during our conversation.

"Perhaps Lieutenant Gray thought I would

"The Beetle Gave Me a Sharp Bite."

change my mind about letting him borrow the beetle if we talked too long—you know how enthusiastic he is on all subjects connected with natural science. So he quickly left, and I must have absent-mindedly put the parchment in my pocket.

"Now, remember when I wanted to sketch the beetle for you, there was no paper on the table. I searched my pockets, hoping to find an old letter or something to draw upon, and my hand came up with the parchment."

"But," I interrupted, "you say that the skull was *not* there when you made the drawing of the beetle."

"I was just coming to that. That's the key to the whole mystery," replied Legrand. "When I gave you the drawing, I watched you carefully until you returned it. And I knew that *you* did not draw the skull."

"Of course not!"

"And no one else could have, either."

"Then how . . . ." I began. But Legrand was

"I Watched You Carefully."

already talking.

"At that point, I made an effort to remember *everything* that took place that afternoon and evening. The weather was chilly—a rare and happy accident—and we had lit the fire. You were seated near it. Just as you were about to inspect my drawing, Wolf entered and leaped upon your shoulders. You petted him and kept him off with your *left* hand, while your *right* hand held the parchment out of his reach. Because of where you were sitting, your *right* hand came very close to the fire. In fact, I recalled that at one moment, I thought the blaze had caught it. But just then Wolf jumped down, and you began to study the sketch.

"When I thought about all these details, it became clear to me that the heat of the fire must have brought out the drawing of the skull. You know that it is possible to write with some chemicals so that the writing cannot be seen until the action of heat or fire

"Your *Right* Hand Came Close to the Fire."

makes the words visible."

"Yes, of course I know that."

"Well, you may not believe this, but I had already made a kind of connection. I had put together two links of a great chain. I had found the remains of an old boat lying along the seacoast, and not far from the boat was the parchment—*not paper*—that Jupiter had used to pick up the beetle."

"But what is the connection?"

"First, you know that the skull, or death's-head, is the well-known emblem of pirates. Their flags . . . ."

"Yes, yes, everyone knows that," I said impatiently.

"Second, parchment is very durable—lasts almost forever. But for the usual kind of drawing or writing, it is not nearly as easy to use as ordinary paper. So parchment would *only* be used for an important message—something that would be kept as a permanent record, something that would not be easily

"I Had Found the Remains of an Old Boat."

damaged. So I concluded that there must be some meaning in the death's-head being drawn on the parchment with some invisible chemical. Then, the size and shape of the parchment supported my idea. Even though one corner was torn off, the original form was oblong—just the size and shape that might have been used for a memorandum—for a record of something to be long remembered and carefully saved."

"But there was no memorandum—only the death's-head," I argued. "I studied it closely."

"So did I," continued Legrand. "I saw that the part of the drawing nearest the edge of the parchment was more distinct than the rest. So the action of the heat must have been uneven. I immediately kindled a fire and held every portion of the parchment over it. At first, some of the lighter lines in the skull became darker. Then, in one corner of the parchment, a small drawing became visible. At first it looked like a goat. Then I looked more

Legrand Held the Parchment over a Fire.

carefully and saw it was a kid."

"Ha! Ha!" I laughed. "To be sure, I have no right to laugh at you—a million and a half of money is not a joke. But you can't make any connection between goats and pirates! Pirates have nothing to do with goats!"

"But I have just said that the figure was a *kid*, not a goat."

"Goats, kids, it's pretty much the same thing."

"Pretty much, but not altogether," replied Legrand. "Of course you've heard of *Captain Kidd*. I realized at once that the animal drawing at the bottom of the parchment was a kind of a punning signature—a humorous way of writing a name. The skull at the top was sort of a seal or letterhead. So that was the third link. But I was most distressed because there was nothing else."

"I suppose you expected to find a letter between the seal and the signature."

"Something like that. The fact is, I had a

The Kid Was a Punning Signature.

feeling of some vast good fortune about to happen. I can't say why. Perhaps, after all, it was more wishful thinking than anything else. And Jupiter's silly words about the bug being of solid gold kept running through my head.

"And then there were the strange co-incidences—that this should all happen on the one fall day in the year which was cool enough for a fire, and that without the fire, without lending the beetle to Lieutenant Gray, or without the dog coming in at that very moment, or indeed, without your unexpected visit, I should never have become aware of the death's-head."

"Go on, please! I can't wait to learn how you figured it out."

"You know all the stories—the thousand vague rumors about Kidd burying money somewhere along the Atlantic coast. Well, I believed that those thousands of rumors must have had some basis. And the fact that the rumors were all so similar and had lasted so

**Did Captain Kidd Bury Money?**

long had to mean that the buried treasure was still buried. Remember, all those stories were about money-*seekers*, not about money-*finders*. If Kidd had hidden the treasure and afterward recovered it, the rumors would not have lasted. Have you ever heard of any important treasure being unearthed along the coast?"

"Never."

"Exactly. So I took it for granted that the earth still held it. Kidd certainly had *intended* to claim his treasure. All the stories about him attest to that. So I decided that some accident must have prevented him from recovering it. This accident must have been known to his followers, who then tried to find it themselves. But they could not, because they had no way of knowing where it was either. Probably it was all this digging and prowling that led to all the rumors in the first place.

"Now, suppose that the reason Kidd did not go back for his treasure was, let us say, the

Stories About Money-*Seekers*

loss of a memorandum indicating its location.'

"And so you guessed . . . ?"

"Exactly—that the parchment I had so strangely found was the lost record of the place of burial."

"But how did you proceed?"

"I held the parchment to the fire again, but nothing happened. I thought that the coating of dirt on it might be in the way, so I carefully rinsed the parchment in warm water and placed it in a pan over lighted charcoal. In a few minutes I saw . . . just what you see now."

"I Saw . . . Just What You See Now."

Legrand Hands Me the Parchment.

# The Gold-Bug

## PART 4

## Cracking Captain Kidd's Code

Legrand had been heating the parchment again as he spoke, and now he handed it to me. A group of mysterious symbols in a reddish ink was neatly arranged in the center of the parchment between the skull and the goat:

53‡‡†305))6*;4826)4‡!)4‡);806*;48†8¶60
))85;1‡(;:‡*8†83(88)5*†;46(;88*96*?;8)*
‡(;485);5*†2:*‡(;4956*2(5*—4)8¶8*;40
69285);)6†8)4‡‡;1(‡9;48081;8:8‡1;48†85;
4)485†528806*81(‡9;48;(88;4(‡?34;48)4
‡;161;:188;‡?;

"But," I said, as I returned the parchment to him, "I am as much in the dark as ever."

"The solution," answered my friend, "is not as difficult as it seems at first glance. From what I've heard about Kidd, he wasn't a particularly clever man. So I was sure he couldn't have come up with a really complicated code. But even a simple one would appear, to an uneducated sailor hunting for the treasure, to be a complete puzzle."

"And you really solved it?"

"Easily. I have always been interested in such riddles, and I have solved others a thousand times harder. After all, one human being cannot invent a puzzle which other human beings would be unable to solve.

"In all secret writings, the first problem is to discover the *language* of the code. Generally, trial and error is the only way. But here, the signature gave it away immediately. The pun upon the word 'Kidd' occurs only in English. Otherwise, I would have tried French

"I Have Solved Harder Riddles."

and Spanish first, since Kidd was a pirate of the Spanish main.

"Of course, the big problem is that, as you can see, there are no divisions between the words. If there were, it would have been clear that a word of *one* symbol would be *a* or *I*, and a word of two symbols could be *is*, *if*, *it*, *or*, or *he*. But since there were no word divisions, my first step was to count all of the symbols to see which were the most frequent and which, the least frequent. I arranged the symbols into a table, like this:

Of the characters 8   there are   33.

|  |  |
|---|---|
| ; | 26. |
| 4 | 19. |
| ‡ and ) | 16. |
| * | 13. |
| 5 | 12. |
| 6 | 11. |
| ( | 10. |
| † and 1 | 8. |
| 0 | 6. |

Arranging the Symbols into a Table

Of the characters 9 and 2 there are 5.

|          |    |
|----------|----|
| : and 3  | 4. |
| ?        | 3. |
| ¶        | 2. |
| ! and —  | 1. |

"Now in English, the letter *e* occurs most frequently. *E* is so frequent, in fact, that there is practically never a sentence of any length in which it is not the most repeated letter. After that, the next most frequent letters in order are:

*a o i d h n r s t u*
*y c f g l m w b k p q x z.*

"So in this code, I felt I was on very safe ground by assuming that the 8 represents *e*. There's an easy way to check this out. *E* is very often doubled in English—in such words as *meet*, *fleet*, *speed*, *agree*, and so on. No other letter is doubled so often."

"The Letter *E* Occurs Most Frequently."

"Aha!" I said, following his explanation easily. "I see here that the double-8 appears five times in this message."

"Exactly. So we can be pretty sure 8 is *e*. Now, of all words in the language, *the* is most common. So if there are three symbols repeated several times in the same order, with the last symbol being 8, they probably represent the word *the*."

"And so there are," I said, as excited as though it were my own discovery. "I see six—no, seven such arrangements."

"Yes, the symbols are ;48. So we may assume that ; represents *t*, 4 represents *h*, and 8 represents *e*.

"And now that we have established a single word, we can also establish the beginnings and endings of several other words. Look, for instance, on the fifth line of the message where the combination ;48 occurs and is followed by ;. We know that the ; must be the beginning of the next word. And we already know five of

;48 Represents *The*.

the six symbols after this *the*. They are:

;(88;4.

"We know that ; is *t*. We don't know (. And we know that 88 is *ee* and 4 is *h*. If we write them down, leaving a space for the one unknown letter, we have:

*t eeth.*

"Now, by trying the entire alphabet, I cannot find any letter to fit the space to make one word ending with *th*. So I assume that the *th* is part of the next word, leaving us:

*t ee.*

"By going through the alphabet, I found that the letter *r* is the best possibility to fill the space after *t*. That gives us:

Leaving a Space for an Unknown Letter

*tree.*

And we learn that *r* is represented by (.

"Looking for the next combination of ;48, we find *the* repeated again seven symbols after *the tree*:

*the tree* ;4(‡?34 *the.*

"Substituting the natural letters where we know them, it looks like this." And he wrote:

*the tree thr‡?3h the.*

As soon as I saw what he had written, I could guess the missing letters—*oug*—*through*, of course. "And so we have three new letters," I said, "*o, u,* and *g*, represented by ‡, ?, and 3. Right?"

"Right. Now let's look through the message for combinations of symbols we know. On the second line of the message, this arrangement

‡?3 Represents *OUG*.

appears:

‡83(88.

"Substituting the letters we know, we get:

†*egree.*

"This looks very much like the word *degree* and gives us another letter, *d*, represented by the symbol †.

"Still on the second line, four symbols beyond the word *degree*, we see the combination:

;46(;88*.

"Substituting the letters we know and leaving a space for the unknown, it looks like this:

*th6rtee*.*

Another Word Begins to Appear.

This immediately suggests the word *thirteen*."

"That gives us two new letters, *i* and *n*, represented by 6 and \*," I cried.

"Correct," said Legrand. "Now look at the very beginning of the message. See the combination:

53‡‡†.

"We know what 3‡‡† are:

5*good*.

"So we can guess that the first letter is *a* and that the first two words of the message are *a good*.

"Now we have quite a few letters, so we can write down our key in a table to avoid confusion." As he spoke, Legrand was writing:

5 represents *a*.  
†     "      *d*.  
8     "      *e*.

Legrand Begins His Table.

| | | |
|---|---|---|
| 3 | represents | *g*. |
| 4 | ,, | *h*. |
| 6 | ,, | *i*. |
| * | ,, | *n*. |
| ‡ | ,, | *o*. |
| ( | ,, | *r*. |
| ; | ,, | *t*. |
| ? | ,, | *u*. |

"We don't have to go any further," he said. "You see for yourself how it works. So here is the full translation of the message." And he handed me these words:

*A good glass in the bishop's hostel in the devil's seat forty-one degrees and thirteen minutes northeast and by north main branch seventh limb east side shoot from the left eye of the death's-head a bee-line from the tree through the shot fifty feet out.*

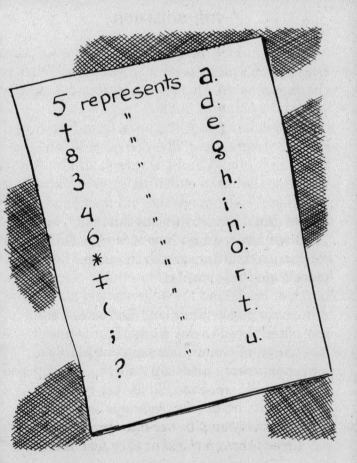

The Table Translates the Message.

"But," I said after reading it, "even this translation still leaves me in the dark. What is the meaning of all this stuff about a *devil's seat* and a *bishop's hostel*?"

"It also left me in the dark for a few days," replied Legrand. "Then I asked all over Sullivan's Island and the mainland about any building that was called 'Bishop's *Hotel*,' for of course I dropped the old-fashioned word *hostel*. But I got no information.

"One morning I got the idea that this might refer to a family named *Bessop*. They have owned an old plantation about four miles north of the island for well over a century. So I went over to the mainland and asked some of the older people who work there. One of the most aged of the women said she had heard of a place known as Bessop's Castle. She agreed to take me there, but said that it was neither a castle, nor a hotel—it was just a high rock.

"I offered to pay her well for her trouble, and we found the spot without much difficulty.

Legrand Questioned an Aged Woman.

Then I sent her back.

"The 'castle' was a cluster of cliffs and rocks, one of them extremely high. I climbed to the top, but then felt completely at a loss. I couldn't imagine what to do next.

"While I stood on that rock thinking it over, my eyes fell upon a narrow ledge on the eastern side of the rock. It was about a yard below me. It stuck out about eighteen inches and was only about a foot wide. The shape of the cliff just above it made it look something like one of those old hollow-backed chairs people used to have."

"The *devil's seat*!" I exclaimed.

"Just what I thought," he answered, "and then the full secret of the riddle dawned on me.

"*A good glass*, I knew, could only be a telescope, for the word *glass* is used that way by sailors. I realized at once that a telescope was to be used from this exact location. The instructions for the angle at which to hold it

At Bessop's Castle

were very precise. The phrases, *forty-one degrees and thirteen minutes* and *northeast and by north* were clearly directions for leveling the telescope. At these discoveries I was, you can be sure, greatly excited. I hurried home, got my telescope, and returned to the rocky cliff at once.

"I let myself down to the ledge and found it was possible to sit upon it in only one position. This confirmed my idea. Then I used the telescope. With my pocket compass I made sure of the *northeast and by north* direction and pointed the glass as nearly at an angle of *forty-one degrees* as I could by guesswork. I moved it cautiously up and down very slowly until I saw a circular opening in the leafy top of the tallest tree in the distance. In the center of this clearing there seemed to be a white spot, but at first I could not make out what it was. I adjusted the focus of the telescope and looked again. It was a human skull!"

"The *death's-head*!" I exclaimed.

Pointing the Telescope at an Angle of 41°

"With this discovery, the puzzle was solved. The phrase *main branch seventh limb east side* could only mean the position of the skull upon the tree. And *shoot from the left eye of the death's-head* had to mean to drop a bullet from the left eye socket of the skull. Then, a *bee-line*, or in other words a straight line, drawn from the nearest point of the trunk *through the shot*, or the spot where the bullet fell, and continued for *fifty feet out*, would indicate a definite point. And I thought it at least possible that beneath this point something of value was hidden."

"This is all quite clear," I said, "although very clever, quite ingenious. When you left the Bessop's Castle, what then?"

"Why, I noted carefully the location of the tree and then went home. But what was most curious was that, the instant I left the devil's seat, I could no longer see the circular opening. Turn as I would, it could not be observed. It seems to me that the cleverest part of the

"The Puzzle Was Solved."

whole thing is the fact that the clearing is visible only from that narrow ledge."

"So we missed the spot the first try at digging," I commented, "because Jupiter let the bug fall through the *right* eye socket instead of the *left*."

"Precisely," he answered. "This mistake made a difference of about two and a half inches in the position of the shot, or peg, nearest the tree. If the treasure had been directly beneath the shot, it wouldn't have mattered. But the shot was one of the two points for setting the line of direction. So while the error was small in the beginning, it increased as we continued along the line. By the time we had gone fifty feet . . . ."

"We were way off the mark," I finished the sentence for him. "But the way you were carrying on! Talking in that dramatic voice! And swinging the beetle—I was sure you were mad! And why did you insist on letting the *bug* fall, instead of a bullet?"

The Bug Fell Through the *Right* Eye Socket.

"Well, to tell you the honest truth, I was quite annoyed by your evident suspicions about my sanity. I resolved to punish you quietly, in my own way, with a little extra mystification. What Jupiter said about the weight of the beetle gave me the idea."

"So that's it," I said. "And now there is only one last thing that still puzzles me. What about the skeletons we found in the pit?"

"I don't know the answer to that any more than you do. But I can guess—although it is dreadful to believe in such an atrocity. It is clear that Kidd would have needed help carrying the box and digging the hole. But after the work was done, he may have decided to cover his tracks completely and do away with all who knew his secret. Perhaps a couple of blows on the head with a pickaxe while his men were busy digging; perhaps it required a dozen blows—who shall tell?"

Indeed, who shall ever tell?

Kidd Killed All Who Knew His Secret.

**ILLUSTRATED CLASSIC EDITIONS**

**EC-EC/D4500-3/1574**